-My Family-
My Single Dad

by Claudia Harrington
illustrated by Zoe Persico

Looking Glass Library

An Imprint of Magic Wagon
abdopublishing.com

To my uncles, aunts, and all of my cousins for being bright, hilarious rays of sunshine whenever I visit home. —ZP

abdopublishing.com

Published by Magic Wagon, a division of ABDO, PO Box 398166, Minneapolis, Minnesota 55439. Copyright © 2018 by Abdo Consulting Group, Inc. International copyrights reserved in all countries. No part of this book may be reproduced in any form without written permission from the publisher. Looking Glass Library™ is a trademark and logo of Magic Wagon.

Printed in the United States of America, North Mankato, Minnesota.
052017
092017

THIS BOOK CONTAINS
RECYCLED MATERIALS

Written by Claudia Harrington
Illustrated by Zoe Persico
Edited by Heidi M.D. Elston
Art Directed by Candice Keimig

Publisher's Cataloging-in-Publication Data

Names: Harrington, Claudia, author. | Persico, Zoe, illustrator.
Title: My single dad / by Claudia Harrington ; illustrated by Zoe
    Persico.
Description: Minneapolis, MN : Magic Wagon, 2018. | Series: My family
Summary: Lenny follows Destiny for a school project and learns what it's like to
    live with a single dad.
Identifiers: LCCN 2017930510 | ISBN 9781532130199 (lib. bdg.) |
    ISBN 9781614798347 (ebook) | ISBN 9781614798415 (Read-to-me ebook)
Subjects: LCSH: Family--Juvenile fiction. | Family life--Juvenile fiction. | Single-
    parent families--Juvenile fiction. | Fathers--Juvenile fiction.
Classification: DDC [E]--dc23
LC record available at http://lccn.loc.gov/2017930510

When the last bell rang, Miss Fish clapped her hands. "Great day, second graders!" She waved the class camera at Lenny. "You're going home with Destiny today. She's Student of the Week."
"Excellent!" said Lenny.
Click!

"How do you get home?" Lenny asked.

Destiny grinned. "Lily picks us up."

"Who's Lily?" Lenny asked.

"My babysitter. She's awesome!"

When Lily pulled up, Destiny slid the door open.
Click!

"Are we stopping at a park?" asked Lenny when they drove along a huge lawn.

"Nope," said Destiny. "Our house is up there."

"Wow!" said Lenny.

Click!

"One sec," Destiny said when they stopped. "I need to finish my art." She pointed at the front door. "Watch!"

8

"Awesome," said Lenny. "Who taught you that?"

Destiny tapped her tablet. "It's Dad's invention."

"Dad?" yelled Destiny when they went in.

"Inside voice," said Lily. "He's finishing a meeting.

I'll be studying."

"You rang?" said Destiny's dad.
"Dad, meet Lenny," said Destiny.
Her dad shook Lenny's hand and
opera music blared.
Lenny gaped. "Is that coming from
my hand?"

"Are buzzers funnier?" asked Destiny's dad.

Destiny giggled. "Dad, can I show Lenny THE ZONE before homework?"

He smiled. "Go ahead and do your homework there. What do you have tonight?"

"We have to invent a new word or word picture," said Destiny.

She led Lenny to a tower on the top floor.
"Wow," said Lenny. "Is this yours?"
Click!

"Not really," said Destiny. "Dad invents stuff. Like this shoe-tying machine. Step on it."

"Whoaaaaa!" said Lenny, looking at his shoes now tied together.

Destiny laughed. "That happens a lot. Dad's fine-tuning it."

Lenny grinned. "Who gets your snack?"

"I do," said Destiny. "Choose your flavor. Then pour a scoop in the top, and press that button."
Click!

"Yum!" said Lenny. "Mango licorice?"
Destiny gave him a thumbs-up.

"Do you always get to do homework here?" asked Lenny.
"Unless Dad has a presentation," said Destiny, handing Lenny a
bucket of markers. "Choose your colors!"

WORDS ROCK, Destiny wrote in the shape of a boulder.

"Word art!" she said proudly.

Click!

FLUBINATOR, wrote Lenny.

"What's that?" asked Destiny.

Lenny grinned. "Something that fixes goofs!"

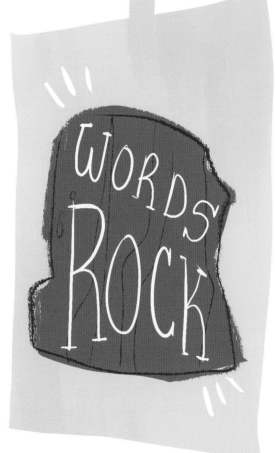

"Let's make self-portraits," said Destiny.

"I need a flubinator," said Lenny, pointing to the nose he drew on the side of his head.

Destiny grinned. "Some artists do that on purpose!"

"Bye, Destiny and Lenny!" called Lily.

"Bye, Lily!" they called back.

"Wait," said Lenny. "What invention makes your dinner?"

Destiny's dad poked his head in. "You're in luck tonight. I made chocolate broccoli."

"Yum," said Lenny.

"Is your hat moving?" Lenny asked.

Click!

"It combs your hair," explained Destiny.

Lenny smoothed his cowlick. "Awesome!"

"Who cleans up the mess?" asked Lenny.

"Everybody!" said Destiny. "Grab a sponge!"

Click!

After cleanup, Destiny showed Lenny her room.

"Watch!" Destiny tapped her tablet.

Her art glowed on the walls.
Click!

"Wow," said Lenny. "Who taught you to draw?"

"My dad," said Destiny. "He's always doodling new inventions."

27

"Who tucks you in?" asked Lenny as his mom peeked in.
"It's just me and Dad. We think up more inventions!
Right before sleep is the best time!"

"Cool," said Lenny. "I think I know this answer, but who loves you best?"

"Me," said her dad. "I couldn't invent a better daughter!"
Click!

Student of the Week

Destiny

WORDS ROCK

"See you tomorrow, word artist," said Lenny as they left.
"Tomorrow, word inventor!" said Destiny.